BY
Lynn Plourde

TEACHER APPRECIATION DAY

ILLUSTRATED BY
Thor Wickstrom

Dutton Children's Books

New York

Text copyright © 2003 by Lynn Plourde
Illustrations copyright © 2003 by Thor Wickstrom
All rights reserved.

CIP Data is available.

Published in the United States by Dutton Children's Books,
a division of Penguin Putnam Books for Young Readers
345 Hudson Street, New York, New York 10014
www.penguinputnam.com

Designed by Irene Vandervoort

Printed in USA
10 9 8 7 6 5 4 3 2 1

First Edition
ISBN 0-525-47113-8

Teacher Appreciation Day was tomorrow.
And everyone in Mrs. Shepherd's class knew *exactly*
how they would show their appreciation to Mrs. Shepherd.
Everyone, that is, except . . .

Maybella Jean Wishywashy.
Maybella couldn't seem to make up her mind,
no matter how hard she tried.

"Eeny meeny miney mo.
So many choices,
I just don't know."

That night at the supermarket, all of the students shopped for a treat to bring in to Mrs. Shepherd. They crowded into the produce aisle and grabbed all kinds of apples—early Macs, late Macs, Red Delicious, Yellow Delicious, Granny Smith, Grampy Smith. As they walked to the checkout line, they all scrubbed, polished, sheened, and shined those apples. They chose apples for Mrs. Shepherd because EVERYONE knows apples are the *official* teacher treat.

Meanwhile, Maybella wandered up and down the store aisles, from the deli to the dairy to the bakery to the pasta to the seafood to the frozen foods. She couldn't make up her mind about a treat for Mrs. Shepherd.

"Eeny meeny miney moos.
So many foods,
how can I choose?"

The next day, when Mrs. Shepherd's students got ready for school, they dressed in green, all shades of green— grassy green, lima-bean green, pickle green, olive green, and leprechaun green. They wore green everything—green pants, green shirts, green dresses, green headbands, green suspenders, green underwear. One girl even painted her freckles green! They all wore green because it was Mrs. Shepherd's favorite color. She'd said so on the first day of school.

Meanwhile, Maybella pulled all of her clothes out
of her dresser and closet. She tried on reddish-oranges
and orangish-reds, greenish-blues and bluish-greens,
pinkish-purples and purplish-pinks, yellowish-golds
and goldish-yellows. She couldn't make up her mind
about a *special* outfit to wear for Mrs. Shepherd.

"Eeny meeny miney mick.
So many colors
that I could pick."

Mrs. Shepherd smiled a super-size smile when her students arrived wearing green, bearing apples, and shouting:

"Happy Teacher Appreciation Day, Mrs. Shepherd."
"You're the best teacher."
"Thanks for being our teacher."
"Hooray for Mrs. Shepherd!"
"Thank you, everyone," said Mrs. Shepherd.
"I love apples."

Then she saw Maybella Jean Wishywashy.

"I couldn't decide which color to wear for you, so I wore everything. And I couldn't decide which treat to bring you, so I brought everything."

"Well, that was very . . . thoughtful of you," answered Mrs. Shepherd.

During morning work time, student after student cleaned the chalkboard for Mrs. Shepherd. They sprayed it, squirted it, swabbed it, and squeegeed it until every single speck of chalk dust had disappeared.

"Thank you, everyone," said Mrs. Shepherd. "It looks great."

Meanwhile, Maybella borrowed paper towels, cleansers, buckets, mops, and a vacuum from the janitor's closet. She couldn't make up her mind which part of the classroom to clean for Mrs. Shepherd.

"Eeny meeny miney mean.
So many places,
what should I clean?"

"I couldn't decide what to clean for you, Mrs. Shepherd, so I cleaned everything," said Maybella.

"Hmm, that was very . . . helpful of you," answered Mrs. Shepherd.

During art, Mrs. Shepherd's students painted special pictures for her. They painted her Irish setter, Sadie. Mrs. Shepherd talked about Sadie all the time —as though she were a kid and not a dog. One day Mrs. Shepherd even brought Sadie to a school picnic. They wore matching baseball caps and sunglasses.

Mrs. Shepherd loved the pictures of Sadie. "Thank you, everyone," she said. "I'll hang these up."

Meanwhile, when Maybella
started to paint Sadie . . .

she thought that Mrs. Shepherd might like kittens, too, or perhaps horses, or maybe gerbils or giraffes, or penguins or puffins, or aardvarks or anteaters, or octopuses or opossums. She couldn't make up her mind about which pet to draw for Mrs. Shepherd.

"Eeny meeny miney mess.
So many pets,
I'll never guess."

"I couldn't decide which pet to paint for you,
Mrs. Shepherd, so I painted every one."
"Er, that was very . . . generous of you,"
said Mrs. Shepherd.

At recess time, students raced around the school-yard field and plucked handfuls of dandelions for Mrs. Shepherd. They didn't have any vases, so they plopped them into cups, caps, and crayon boxes.

"Thank you, everyone," said Mrs. Shepherd. "I'll take these home."

Meanwhile, Maybella raced around the school-yard field looking in holes, spying under rocks, and climbing up trees. She just couldn't make up her mind which nature surprise to bring to Mrs. Shepherd.

"Eeny meeny miney mup.
So much stuff,
I might give up."

"I couldn't decide which beautiful thing to share with you, Mrs. Shepherd, so I brought everything," said Maybella.

"Um, that was very . . . considerate of you," said Mrs. Shepherd.

Later that afternoon, a TV crew from Channel 5 visited Mrs. Shepherd's class.

"We're going to tape a story about Teacher Appreciation Day for tonight's news," announced the crew.

The students tee-heed, giggled, snickered, and sang, "We're going to be on TV! We're going to be on TV!"

But when the camera flashed on and the reporter flicked on his microphone and asked, "What is it you appreciate about your teacher?" all of Mrs. Shepherd's students froze. The reporter moved from student to student with his microphone, but all he got for answers were:

"Er-er-er."

"Ah-ah-ah."

"Um-um-um."

Until he got to Maybella Jean Wishywashy.
Maybella said,

"Eeny meeny miney mide.
So many things . . .

I CAN decide!

"What do I appreciate about Mrs. Shepherd?"
Maybella shouted, "EVERYTHING!"

And she ran to give Mrs. Shepherd a super-size hug.

"My, that was very ... decisive, Maybella.
I appreciate you, too," said Mrs. Shepherd as she
returned Maybella's super-size hug.

Later that night, Mrs. Shepherd saw the whole thing on the evening news.

"It sure is nice to be appreciated," she said with a smile. "But once a year is quite enough!"